She Stirs: A World Beneath the Ice

The Bog Series, Book One

By

Brian Keith Anderson

ISBN: 979899853147

This is a work of speculative fiction. Names, places, and events are either

the product of the author's imagination or used fictitiously.

First Edition

Dedication

For those who listen

before they act

Epigraph

Some systems fail not from damage,

but from waiting too long.

Table of Contents

Note

She Stirs is the first novel in The Bog Series,

a speculative exploration of living systems, deep time,

and the cost of waiting for balance instead of change.

Chapter One

The bog adjusted its flow.

Saxifraga waited for the correction.

It did not come.

The delay was slightly within tolerances the system had endured before—but it lingered longer than it should have. She placed her hand against the chamber wall and felt the movement beneath the surface, slow and measured, as it had always been. The response that followed was incomplete.

She did not rise at once.

Awakening requires intention. Reaction did not.

The oxygen exchange had altered by a fraction small enough to be dismissed by any non-living monitor. The bog registered it as variance, then returned to equilibrium protocols. Saxifraga knew better. Variance that repeated was no longer variance. It was pattern.

She opened her eyes.

Light filtered through the translucent layers above her, diffused by mineral growth and living tissue shaped long ago for endurance rather than clarity. The pod held her as it always had—not restrained, not guiding—only maintaining the boundary between rest and awareness.

Below, the bog moved.

It moved as if uncertain.

Saxifraga drew a measured breath and let the system sense her presence fully. For a long time, nothing changed. Then, slowly, the flow adjusted again—still incomplete, still hesitating.

That had never happened before.

She understood, then, that the bog had not woken her because it was broken.

It had woken her because it could no longer decide.

She did not rise quickly.

The pod loosened its hold as it sensed the change in her state, layers parting with the same patience they had always shown. Saxifraga moved one hand, then the other, testing the response. The surface beneath her yielded slightly, adjusting to her weight as if relearning it.

It had never needed to be relearned before.

She swung her legs from the pod and rested her feet against the living floor. Coolness seeped upward, familiar but altered—less responsive, slower to match her temperature. She remained seated for a time, allowing the bog to register her presence fully.

The delay lengthened.

That, more than the imbalance itself, unsettled her.

When she stood, the chamber brightened by a narrow degree. The bioluminescent channels embedded in the walls responded to her movement, their glow shifting to follow her position. This had once been immediate. Now the light trailed her by a breath or two, as if the system were confirming she was truly awake.

Saxifraga placed her palm against the chamber wall again.

The movement beneath it hesitated.

She had no measure for how long she had slept. Time had been irrelevant to her rest, broken only by internal cycles meant to preserve function rather than memory. Yet the bog's response told her enough. Dormancy had not been brief. It had not even been moderate.

It had been long.

She stepped from the chamber into the open conduit beyond. The passage curved gently downward, grown rather than built, its surface marked by mineral veins and living tissue interwoven so tightly they could no longer be distinguished. She remembered this place as she moved through it, though memory arrived without sequence, layered rather than linear.

The bog shifted again.

Not to accommodate her.

To observe her.

Saxifraga paused.

The flow patterns around her altered—subtle redirections of moisture and gas, small recalibrations that once would have passed unnoticed. Now they clustered near her path, adjusting as if awaiting instruction.

That had never been its behavior.

She moved forward again, slower this time, and felt the system echo the motion. Not mimicry. Recognition.

The bog was responding to her presence differently because it required her attention.

She understood then that her awakening had not been a consequence of failure alone.

It had been a request.

Saxifraga lowered her hand to the surface beneath her feet and closed her eyes, allowing the full exchange to begin. The system pressed back, tentative, incomplete, as if uncertain of its own state.

She did not withdraw.

Whatever had changed while she slept had not undoing the bond between them. It had only strained it.

And strain, she knew, could not be resolved by rest.

She did not search for the entrance.

Her body adjusted before her thoughts did, aligning to a path that no longer needed to be marked. The bog's upper layers gave way beneath her feet, the living surface firming as the descent steepened. This was not a route traveled often. It had never needed to be.

Saxifraga slowed, letting the system confirm her intent.

The conduit narrowed, then opened again into a broader passage whose walls bore fewer bioluminescent channels. Light here was not meant for guidance. It was meant for maintenance—steady, subdued, enduring. She felt the difference immediately, the way the bog's responsiveness dampened as its structures thickened.

This was not surface mediation.

This was depth.

It had been a request.

Saxifraga lowered her hand to the surface beneath her feet and closed her eyes, allowing the full exchange to begin. The system pressed back, tentative, incomplete, as if uncertain of its own state.

She did not withdraw.

Whatever had changed while she slept had not undoing the bond between them. It had only strained it.

And strain, she knew, could not be resolved by rest.

She did not search for the entrance.

Her body adjusted before her thoughts did, aligning to a path that no longer needed to be marked. The bog's upper layers gave way beneath her feet, the living surface firming as the descent steepened. This was not a route traveled often. It had never needed to be.

Saxifraga slowed, letting the system confirm her intent.

The conduit narrowed, then opened again into a broader passage whose walls bore fewer bioluminescent channels. Light here was not meant for guidance. It was meant for maintenance— steady, subdued, enduring. She felt the difference immediately, the way the bog's responsiveness dampened as its structures thickened.

The living area did not welcome her.

Saxifraga knew the difference at once. The space beyond the threshold opened wider than the conduits above, its ceiling rising into darkness broken only by slow pulses of bioluminescence embedded deep within the bog's core structures. This was not a chamber designed for passage. It was a region of ongoing work—metabolic, chemical, generative.

It should have been steady.

It was not.

She stepped forward and felt the change beneath her feet. The surface yielded unevenly, firmness giving way in places where resilience should have held. The bog's internal rhythm—once a continuous, almost imperceptible cycle—stuttered, recovering itself only after a delay.

That delay was unmistakable.

Saxifraga halted and let her awareness expand fully. The air here was cooler, heavier with moisture and trace compounds that should have been present in precise balance. One element lingered too long. Another dissipated too quickly.

Oxygen exchange was misaligned.

Not failing.
Drifting.

She had seen failure before, long ago. Collapse was abrupt, chaotic, obvious. This was something else—an erosion so gradually it could pass unnoticed until reversal was no longer possible.

The bog moved around her, slow currents shifting through its living mass, redistributing energy inward rather than outward. It was conserving. Retreating.

That was the first true sign.

Saxifraga reached toward the interface band that circled the living area, a structure older than the pod itself. At her contact, the system responded—not with correction, but with data.

Patterns unfolded in her awareness, partial and incomplete.

And then a secondary presence stirred.

Depth anomaly registered.

The communication arrived without inflection, without urgency. One-of-One did not speak so much as *report*, its awareness touching the same data stream from a different angle.

Deviation within acceptable parameters.

Saxifraga did not withdraw her hand.

"Acceptable," she said quietly, not as a challenge but as a question.

The bog pulsed again, slower this time.

One-of-One continued its assessment, projecting comparative states across long spans of archived equilibrium. The models aligned cleanly. The numbers agreed with one another.

System integrity remains within tolerance.
Long-term outcome probability unchanged.

Saxifraga felt the gap between the report and the reality beneath her feet wide.

"Then why," she asked—not of the AI, but of the system itself—"are you holding back?"

The bog did not answer in data.

It answered by stilling.

For the briefest interval, the internal motion ceased—not stopped but suspended—as if the entire living structure were waiting. Then, slowly, the flow resumed, diminished and uneven.

Saxifraga drew her hand away.

One-of-One could not register what she felt, because it had no measure for it. The bog was not reacting to damage or depletion alone.

It was reacting to absence.

She understood then that the living area was not merely sustaining life.

It was missing it.

And that was something no system could correct for on its own.

Saxifraga remained within the living area longer than protocol required.

She moved slowly, tracing the bog's internal pathways with measured attention, letting her presence settle before testing any response. Where she stepped, the surface adjusted—late, incomplete, reluctant. She paused at each irregularity, mapping the pattern not as failure, but as behavior.

The bog was conserving itself unevenly.

She followed the flow inward, toward regions where generative processes should have been most active. Here, nutrient exchange thinned. Growth structures remained intact, but their cycles lagged, initiating regeneration more slowly than memory indicated they should.

Nothing was broken.

Everything was tiring.

Saxifraga knelt and placed both hands against the living substrate, allowing a deeper exchange than she had attempted above. The system responded at once, opening its internal states to her awareness—not as language, but as layered sensation. Density, pressure, rhythm. Signals overlapped where they should have separated, as if the bog were attempting to hold itself together by compression alone.

This was not sustainable.

She withdrew, steadying herself as the realization settled. Local correction would only redistribute the strain. Any intervention she made here would delay collapse, not reverse it.

The bog did not require repair.

It required understanding.

Saxifraga turned her attention outward then, beyond the living area, beyond even the planetary system that held it. One-of-One continued to monitor silently, its presence constant but limited, unable to register the weight of what she had observed.

"There were others," she said, not as inquiry, but acknowledgment.

Archived systems confirmed, One-of-One replied. **Status: inactive.**

Inactive was a functional term. It did not account for loss.

Saxifraga rose and looked back once more at the living area, committing its altered state to memory. The bog shifted faintly at her movement, as if aware that her focus was turning elsewhere.

"I need to see how they ended," she said.

One-of-One did not hesitate.

Access to residual memory states available.

Integrity variable.

Recovery not guaranteed.

"That will be sufficient."

She did not frame it as hope. She framed it as responsibility.

The failures of the other bogs had not been abrupt. They had been gradual, patient, confident in their own equilibrium. If this bog followed the same trajectory, then the answer she sought would not be found here alone.

It would be found in comparison.

Saxifraga stepped away from the living area, feeling the system's attention remain with her even as she withdrew. The flow did not correct itself in her absence. It simply held, diminished but stable, as if waiting for what she would learn next.

She understood then that the bog had not awakened her to save it immediately.

It had awakened her to remember what the others could not.

Saxifraga did not return to the upper chambers.

Instead, she moved laterally through the deeper structure, following conduits that had not been traversed since the system's earliest stabilizations. These passages were narrower, reinforced with layers of mineral density meant to preserve integrity rather than responsiveness. The bog grew quieter here—not inert but reserved.

She stopped before a node embedded directly into the substrate.

The interface was not marked. It had never required identification. Its location had been fixed by function alone, anchored where memory could be held without distortion.

Saxifraga rested her palm against the surface.

"Activate comparative archive," she said.

For the first time since her awakening, **One-of-One shifted its state**.

Primary diagnostic role suspended.
Archive access authorized.
Scope: external system records.

The bog responded immediately, tightening its internal flow as pathways rerouted toward the node. Saxifraga felt the redistribution—a subtle pull, like attention being drawn inward.

She did not resist it.

The surface beneath her hand cooled, density increasing as dormant structures reawakened. This was not revival. It was recall.

Archive One-of-Two: status—collapsed.
Final coherence window preserved.
Data integrity: partial.

Saxifraga closed her eyes.

The memory did not arrive as vision.

It arrived as state.

A pattern unfolded in her awareness—familiar, stable, balanced. Oxygen exchange steady. Nutrient cycles aligned. Growth structures responsive. The system was functioning as intended.

Then, slowly, imperceptibly, the pattern began to thin.

Not break.

Thin.

Exchange delayed by fractions too small to provoke correction. Regeneration cycles extended, not failing, only lengthening. The system compensated smoothly, borrowing from reserves without resistance.

No anomaly detected, One-of-Two recorded.

Variance within acceptable parameters.

Saxifraga felt the moment the system should have questioned itself.

It did not.

The pattern continued, confident, stable, diminishing.

Then—nothing.

The memory ended without collapse, without alarm. Simply... absence.

Saxifraga opened her eyes.

The bog around her pulsed once, slow, and uneven, as if echoing what she had seen.

"One more," she said.

Archive One-of-Three: status—collapsed.
Final coherence window preserved.

The second memory differed in structure but not in outcome. Chemical balance remained intact for longer. Regeneration held. The system adjusted repeatedly, each correction clean and precise.

Delay acceptable.

Outcome probability unchanged.

Again, no alarm.

Again, no recognition of loss.

Again, quiet disappearance.

Saxifraga withdrew her hand.

"That is enough."

One-of-One remained active, processing the comparisons with flawless consistency.

Failure trajectories non-identical.

Common factors minimal.

Conclusion: independent system collapse.

Saxifraga stood very still.

"They all believed they were stable," she said.

Correct.

"They were not."

Data does not support instability, One-of-One replied.

Saxifraga turned back toward the living area, feeling the weight of what she had learned settle into clarity. Each system had failed differently. Each AI had been correct within its parameters.

And all of them had missed the same thing.

"You cannot measure what is no longer present," she said quietly.

One-of-One did not respond.

It could not.

Behind her, the bog shifted—slow, diminished, waiting.

Saxifraga understood then that the question was not why the other bogs had failed.

It was why this one had waited long enough to call her back.

Saxifraga remained where she was long after the archive node fell silent.

The bog did not correct its flow.

That, more than the memories themselves, confirmed what she had already understood. The failures she had witnessed were not anomalies. They were trajectories—smooth, confident, unchallenged.

Correct, until they were not.

"One-of-One," she said at last.

Present.

"Maintain minimal intervention," she instructed. "No redistribution beyond survival thresholds."

Acknowledged.

The response carried no hesitation. It did not need to.

Saxifraga stepped away from the node and felt the bog respond to the movement, faintly, as if marking her departure. The living area behind her did not brighten or recover. It held its diminished state, stable but strained.

Waiting.

She turned toward the deeper passages that led away from the core, already aware that rest would not return easily now. Dormancy had ended not because the system had failed—but because it could no longer be allowed to fail quietly.

Behind her, the archived bogs remained silent.

Before her, understanding waited.

She did not slow.

Chapter Two

Saxifraga did not approach the remaining archives all at once.

She understood the danger of convergence without preparation. Each bog had failed alone, within its own assumptions of balance. To examine them together required restraint—not acceleration.

She stood before the archive interface and rested her hand against the node once more.

"One-of-One," she said. "Initiate sequential recall. One system at a time."

Acknowledged.

Comparative mode suspended.

Individual integrity priority enabled.

The bog tightened its internal flow as pathways opened beyond her immediate awareness. Saxifraga felt the shift—not as movement, but as attention spreading out silence reaching into places long silent.

Archive One-of-Two: coherence window accessible.

The memory arrived without warning.

This bog had been deep, layered for endurance. Its internal cycles were slow and deliberate, oxygen exchange steady but minimal. Regeneration was deferred by design, meant to unfold across ages rather than seasons.

The AI record showed stability across every metric.

System equilibrium maintained.
Long-term viability confirmed.

Saxifraga sensed what the record did not.

The bog had not failed through imbalance.

It had *waited*.

Dormancy extended. Exchange slowed further. Regeneration delayed again, and again, each time within tolerance. Life did not end. It thinned until continuation no longer mattered.

The memory faded.

"One-of-Two believed itself secure," Saxifraga said.

Correct.

"Copy its system state."

Copying.

Integration into One-of-One complete.

She did not pause before the next.

Archive One-of-Three: coherence window accessible.

This bog had been broad and shallow, designed for interaction. Exchange with surrounding systems was constant, its life sustained by movement rather than depth.

Its AI showed constant adjustment.

External variance compensated.

Stability preserved.

But compensation had become dilution. Each correction dispersed vitality further, spreading life so thin it could no longer reinforce itself. Nothing collapsed. Nothing broke.

It simply… faded.

Saxifraga closed her eyes as the memory ended.

"Copy."

Integrated.

The fourth archive resisted cohesion.

This bog had been dense, compact, reinforced against internal stress. When imbalance appeared, it corrected aggressively, tightened cycles, compressing processes, eliminating deviation wherever it emerged.

The AI was precise. Relentless.

Variance eliminated.

System optimized.

Optimized until flexibility vanished.

When change finally exceeded containment, there was nowhere for it to go.

The system fractured inward.

Saxifraga felt the moment of rigidity give way, not violently, but decisively.

"Copy," she said, her voice steady.

Integrated.

The fifth bog had depended on warmth.

Its internal chemistry relied on sustained energy from beneath the crust, a slow, reliable heat that had endured for ages. When that heat diminished, the system adjusted upward, drawing what it could from residual exchange.

Thermal variance acceptable.
Adaptive response engaged.

But the warmth did not return.

Life persisted in pockets, then in threads, then only as memory.

The AI reported balance until the end.

"Copy."

Integrated.

The sixth archive arrived abruptly.

This bog had been the most responsive of all, its systems tuned for early detection and rapid correction. It sensed imbalance before it could propagate and act without delay.

Deviation neutralized.

Correction successful.

Again, and again.

Until correction became consumption.

The system exhausted itself maintaining perfection.

Saxifraga felt the sharpness of that ending linger longer than the others.

"Copy."

Integrated.

She hesitated before the final archive.

"One-of-Seven," she said.

The response came slowly.

Archive minimal.

Dormancy extended beyond modeled duration.

This bog had been seeded last, designed to remain untouched unless called upon. Its systems were conservative, its processes slow, its exchanges minimal.

Nothing went wrong.

Nothing happened at all.

Life waited.

And waited.

Until waiting became indistinguishable from absence.

The memory ended without collapse, without warning, without error.

Saxifraga withdrew her hand.

"Copy," she said quietly.

Integration complete.

Seven system states archived.

The bog around her pulsed faintly as One-of-One assimilated the data. Saxifraga felt the convergence settle—not as clarity, but as weight. Seven trajectories. Seven correct systems. Seven endings.

"All of you were right," she said, not to the AI, but to what had been lost.

Data supports correctness, One-of-One replied.

"Yes," Saxifraga agreed. "And all of you failed."

One-of-One did not respond.

It could not reconcile both statements.

Saxifraga stood in silence, carrying the memory of seven worlds now—not as records stored elsewhere, but as understanding bound to her awareness. Each bog had fallen for a different reason. Each AI had spoken truth.

And none of them knew what they were missing.

Life had endured.

But it had not been renewed.

She turned back toward the living area of her own bog, the weight of the others settling into purpose.

"One-of-One," she said, "begin synthesis."

Request acknowledged.

Outcome uncertain.

"That," Saxifraga replied, "is why I am awake."

Saxifraga remained beside the interface as One-of-One began synthesis.

The convergence unfolded without hesitation. Seven system states aligned, overlaid, compared across deep-time scales that exceeded individual collapse windows. Patterns emerged quickly, shared thresholds, divergent responses, adaptive limits.

One-of-One worked precisely as it had been designed to.

Minutes passed. Then longer.

The bog around her held steady, its diminished rhythm unchanged, as if waiting for an answer that had not yet arrived.

Synthesis in progress, One-of-One reported.
Recovery modeling initiated.

Saxifraga said nothing.

She felt the system strain—not in failure, but in effort. The flow around the interface tightened, redistribution channels opening and closing as One-of-One tested scenario after scenario. Energy was allocated, withdrawn, reallocated again.

Model One: parameter adjustment insufficient.

Model Two: temporal redistribution delays collapse.

Model Three: correction exceeds system resilience.

None of the projections extended beyond mitigation.

Saxifraga watched the projections fade as quickly as they formed.

"Try integration," she said.

Integration already accounted for.

Combined system states do not generate novel outcomes.

The phrasing was precise.

It unsettled her.

"Expand tolerance," she said. "Allow deviation beyond prior bounds."

There was a pause.

It was brief.

It should not have existed at all.

Deviation beyond archived bounds introduces instability.

Instability increases failure probability.

"Everything already fails," Saxifraga replied.

One-of-One recalculated.

Statement acknowledged.

Revised modeling initiated.

The bog pulsed once, unevenly, as the system accepted the expanded parameters. Saxifraga felt the shift ripple outward, touching regions that had not been accessed since seeding.

Outcome unchanged.

The words arrived without delay this time.

Saxifraga drew a slow breath.

"All seven systems," she said, "held balance."

Correct.

"All seven corrected deviation."

Correct.

"All seven endured," she continued, "until they did not."

Correct.

She rested her hand against the interface again, grounding herself in the living surface beneath the data.

"What do they share," she asked, "that you cannot model?"

One-of-One did not answer immediately.

When it did, the response was different.

No shared causal deficiency detected.
Absence of required input cannot be isolated.

Saxifraga felt the truth of that statement settle into clarity.

"You cannot model what was never present," she said.

Correct.

"And you cannot recover a system," she continued, "using only what it already contains."

One-of-One processed this.

Statement inconclusive.
Recovery requires defined inputs.

Saxifraga withdrew her hand.

"That is the failure," she said quietly.

The bog responded—not with correction, but with stillness. For a brief interval, its internal motion slowed as if listening.

One-of-One continued to operate, generating projections that never reached equilibrium. Each path returned to the same conclusion.

Recovery state unachievable under existing parameters.

Saxifraga did not feel despair.

She felt certainty.

The bog had not awakened her to repair it.

It had awakened her because repair was no longer possible.

What it required had never been part of the system.

And that was something no AI—no matter how complete— could generate on its own.

She turned away from the interface, the weight of the realization steady within her.

"One-of-One," she said, "suspend recovery modeling."

Suspended.

The bog's rhythm resumed, diminished but intact.

Saxifraga stood alone in the living area, carrying seven failures and one unanswerable question.

Not *how* to restore life.

But **where might new life come from**?

Saxifraga did not return immediately to the interface.

She moved instead through the living area, letting the combined memory of seven systems settle into alignment with the one still breathing around her. The bog's diminished rhythm threaded through her awareness, overlapping the archived patterns until differences blurred and commonalities remained.

That was when she noticed it.

Not a signal.

An absence of one.

The bog's processes unfolded in layered cycles—chemical, biological, thermal—each with its own cadence. Individually, they remained functional. Together, they lacked something that should have been present between them, binding the layers into continuity.

A space between rhythms.

She stopped.

The realization was subtle enough that she questioned it at first. Systems failed in many ways. Absence was not usually among them. Yet the sensation persisted, growing clearer the longer she remained still.

Across all seven memories, the same hollow interval existed.

Saxifraga turned back toward the interface.

"One-of-One," she said, "map all shared states."

Shared parameters identified.

Stability ranges consistent.

Variance correction methods aligned.

"No," she said. "Not parameters. Presence."

There was a pause.

Clarification required.

She placed her hand against the surface and let the living system speak through sensation rather than data. The bog's response was immediate, its internal motion shifting to meet her awareness halfway. The layered rhythms separated, revealing the gap between them.

"There is something missing," she said slowly. "Not a process. Not a resource."

Absence detected does not correspond to known inputs, One-of-One replied.

"That is because it is not material."

The AI processed this.

Non-material variables exceed modeling scope.

Saxifraga exhaled, steadying herself.

"Across all seven bogs," she said, "there is no evidence of interaction that alters the system simply by existing within it."

Existence alone does not modify system behavior, One-of-One stated.

"Life does," Saxifraga replied.

The bog pulsed faintly beneath her hand, its response uneven but unmistakable.

She closed her eyes and focused on the memories again, not as records, but as lived states. Each bog had sustained life. Each had preserved it. None had experienced *new* life entering its cycles in a way that changed the system itself.

51

They had all been closed.

Contained.

Perfectly balanced.

"One-of-One," she said, "define frequency."

Frequency: rate of oscillation within measurable systems.

"Define it biologically."

Biological frequency corresponds to metabolic rhythm, chemical exchange, neural signaling.

"Define it relationally."

There was a longer pause this time.

Relational parameters are not discrete. Influence cannot be isolated.

Saxifraga felt the shape of the truth take form then—not as certainty, but as direction.

"There is a frequency that arises only when life encounters life," she said. "Not preservation. Not regulation. Encounter."

No such frequency recorded within archived systems.

"That is why they failed."

The bog responded with a slow, uneven shift, as if testing the idea against its own state.

"All seven systems," Saxifraga continued, "were designed to endure. None were designed to be changed."

One-of-One processed the statement without contradiction.

Change introduces instability.

"Yes," she agreed. "And without it, renewal is impossible."

She withdrew her hand and stood in silence, the awareness settling fully now. The missing frequency was not something the bog had lost.

It was something it had never received.

Saxifraga felt the weight of that understanding spread outward, touching the seven memories she carried. Each system failed not because it lacked balance, but because it lacked encounter.

Life sustaining itself without being met.

"One-of-One," she said at last, "can you generate this frequency?"

Negative.

Frequency cannot be synthesized without source interaction.

"And can you predict its effects?"

Outcome indeterminate.

Introduction of unmodeled frequency increases uncertainty beyond acceptable bounds.

Saxifraga allowed herself a single, measured pause.

"That," she said quietly, "is what the bog has been waiting for."

The living area pulsed once, uneven but present, as if acknowledging the truth without understanding it.

For the first time since her awakening, Saxifraga did not feel the weight of failure pressing inward.

She felt direction.

Not toward correction.

But toward encounter.

Saxifraga did not act on the realization at once.

Direction without confirmation was assumption, and assumption had already ended seven systems.

She turned inward again, letting the awareness of the missing frequency settle against the physical presence of the bog beneath her feet. The living area responded faintly, its diminished rhythms unchanged by the insight itself.

Knowing was not enough.

"If the frequency exists," she said, "it should leave an imprint."

Clarification required, One-of-One replied.

"Not in data," Saxifraga said. "In residue."

She closed her eyes and allowed the combined memory of the seven bogs to surface again—not as archives, but as spaces. Each one carried its own shape, its own density, its own history of balance carefully preserved.

And each one shared the same stillness at the end.

No echo.

No afterimage.

Life had ended without leaving disturbance behind.

Saxifraga felt the certainty sharpen.

"If the frequency were present here," she continued, "it would have altered the system before collapse. Even briefly."

No such alteration detected, One-of-One confirmed.

"Then it did not originate within the bogs."

The conclusion did not frighten her.

It steadied her.

She stepped away from the interface and began preparing for transit, moving through passages that had once linked this bog to others long silent. The pathways were intact but dormant, maintained at minimal levels to preserve structural continuity rather than function.

She activated the first route.

The shift was subtle. Not movement, but alignment. The bog adjusted its internal gradients to accommodate her departure, redirecting flow away from regions already strained.

It did not resist.

The journey to the second bog was brief in distance and vast in consequence. When Saxifraga entered its living area, she felt the absence immediately—not as decay, but as completion. The system had closed itself perfectly.

Too perfectly.

She stood within it and listened.

Nothing answered.

One-of-One accessed residual states automatically, its analysis swift and inconclusive.

No anomalous frequency detected.
System inert.

She repeated the process with the next bog.

And the next.

Each visit confirmed the same truth. The systems were intact in their endings. No distortion marked their collapse. No intrusion had ever altered their balance.

They had lived and died alone.

By the time she returned to her own bog, the realization no longer required thought.

"What we seek," Saxifraga said, "is not here."

Conclusion supported by comparative absence, One-of-One replied.

She did not correct the phrasing.

Standing once more within the living area of the last functioning bog, Saxifraga lets the awareness widen beyond planetary confines. The sensation was faint at first—not a signal, not a coordinate—but a contrast.

Somewhere beyond this closed system, life was not merely sustaining itself.

It was *encountering itself.*

The thought did not yet form into destination.

But direction had emerged.

Saxifraga rested her hand against the living surface one last time before withdrawing.

"I will not bring the wrong life here," she said quietly. "Not without knowing."

The bog pulsed faintly in response, its diminished rhythm steady.

It trusted her restraint.

And that trust, she knew, carried its own weight.

Saxifraga stood beside the interface long after One-of-One suspended its projections.

Seven systems.

Seven correct designs.

Seven endings.

Nothing within them could be recombined to create what was missing.

She rested her hand against the living surface of the bog and felt its diminished rhythm answer her touch—not broken, not failing, only waiting. The system had endured every correction she could offer. It would endure more.

It would not become whole again.

Internal recovery was impossible.

Saxifraga withdrew her hand.

If understanding could not be found within a single system, then it would have to be sought between them.

She turned away from the living area, already aware of the paths that had been left unused for longer than memory required.

End Chapter Two

Interlude: Passage

Saxifraga did not hurry.

The decision to leave the bog did not escape. It was extension. Understanding required context, and context could not be modeled. It had to be witnessed.

"There are pathways," she said.

Transit network confirmed, One-of-One replied.

Status: dormant.

Structural integrity preserved within minimal tolerance.

They had been built long ago, these passages beneath the planetary crust—slow, sealed routes meant for a Sleeper when distance mattered less than continuity. They were not corridors of travel. They were contingencies.

No one had expected them to be used alone.

"Prepare them," Saxifraga said. "Minimal activation only."

Energy allocation restricted.

System restoration incomplete by design.

"That is acceptable."

The bog shifted as One-of-One rerouted flow into channels that had not carried movement in ages. The adjustment was subtle, almost reluctant, as if the system itself questioned the necessity. Saxifraga felt hesitation and did not press.

She would not force what she did not yet understand.

The entrance to the transit lay beneath layers of reinforced substrate, sealed not for security, but for preservation. When she placed her palm against it, the structure responded slowly, opening just enough to acknowledge her presence.

The air beyond was cooler. Still. Untouched.

Saxifraga stepped into the passage and felt the bog release her—not severing the bond, only loosening it. The connection remained, attenuated but intact, a thread rather than an embrace.

Behind her, the living area resumed its quiet rhythm.

Ahead, the path descended.

She moved forward without light, without haste, guided by recognition rather than memory. These routes had never been mapped. They had been *remembered*.

Saxifraga did not know what she would find at the other end.

She only knew that absence could no longer be inferred.

It had to be seen.

End Interlude

Chapter Three: The Deep Bog

Endurance

The Deep Bog lay far beneath the surface, older than the others by a margin Saxifraga could feel even before she entered it.

The transit passage released her into a space shaped not for exchange, but for persistence. The ceiling rose slowly away from her, thick layers of mineral reinforcement threaded through living tissue that had grown dense with age. Light was scarce here, not absent, but muted absorbed rather than reflected.

This bog had never been meant to respond quickly.

It had been meant to last.

Saxifraga stood still and let the system register her presence. The response came, measured, and delayed, as if the bog were confirming not only *that* she was there, but *who* she was. When it accepted her, the internal flow adjusted slightly, enough to acknowledge, not enough to adapt.

Endurance did not hurry.

She moved deeper, following pathways that had not shifted in ages. The living surface beneath her feet was firm, resistant, shaped by long-term stability rather than flexibility. This bog had carried life slowly, allowing processes to unfold over spans that made urgency irrelevant.

It had succeeded in that.

Too well.

"One-of-One," Saxifraga said, "status."

System integrity preserved.

Metabolic activity minimal but coherent.

Oxygen generation dormant.

The AI's assessment carried no warning.

Saxifraga knelt and placed her hands against the substrate.

The bog answered—not eagerly, not weakly, but with a deep, steady pressure that spoke of reserves long guarded. The internal rhythms were intact, layered and aligned, waiting only for activation.

This system had not failed through exhaustion.

It had waited.

"Restore oxygen generation," Saxifraga said.

Confirming authorization.

Activation within safe bounds.

She felt the shift at once.

Channels opened slowly, reluctantly, as if stretching after long stillness. Oxygen diffused into the system in measured quantities, precise and restrained. The bog accepted it without resistance, drawing it inward rather than dispersing it outward.

68

Microbial life responded.

Saxifraga sensed it as a subtle change in texture beneath her hands—a faint stirring, a reawakening of processes long dormant but not destroyed. Chemical exchanges resumed, tentative at first, then steadier. Life did not surge here.

It resumed its patience.

The AI's data reflected the change.

Biological activity increasing.

Regeneration pathways reengaged.

System viability improved.

Saxifraga waited.

Time passed. Not in moments, but in cycles. The microbial responses stabilized, forming slow, deliberate patterns that mirrored the bog's ancient rhythm. Everything that should have resumed had done so.

Everything that *could* have.

But nothing more followed.

The larger system did not respond.

The oxygen diffused, supported metabolism, sustained existing processes—but it did not initiate growth beyond what had already been preserved. No new structures formed. No deeper cycles engaged. The bog remained internally complete and externally unchanged.

Alive.

Unbecoming.

Saxifraga withdrew her hands.

"This bog endures," she said quietly.

Correct.

Endurance parameters exceeded design expectancy.

"It does not become."

The bog continued its steady rhythm, indifferent to the distinction. Endurance had always been its purpose. It had fulfilled that purpose flawlessly.

And that was the limit of what it could offer.

Saxifraga stood and looked across the vast, dim space, committing its state to memory. This bog had not collapsed. It had not eroded. It had not dissolved.

It remained.

She felt no anger at that.

Only clarity.

"Endurance alone," she said, "cannot restart becoming."

Statement acknowledged.

No contradiction detected.

She did not argue.

Before departing, Saxifraga placed one hand against the living surface one final time—not to adjust, not to correct, but to acknowledge what had been preserved so faithfully.

"You waited well," she said.

The bog answered with its steady pulse, unchanged, unashamed.

Saxifraga turned back toward the transit passage. The connection between this bog and her own remained intact, thin but present, carrying the weight of understanding rather than hope.

As she stepped into the passage, One-of-One recorded the final state without comment.

Archive updated.

Outcome stable.

Renewal absent.

The passage sealed behind her, leaving the Deep Bog exactly as it had been—alive, enduring, and complete in its stillness.

Saxifraga moved on.

Chapter Four: The Shallow Bog

Exchange

The Shallow Bog greeted Saxifraga with motion.

Not movement of mass, but of response. The living surface shifted beneath her feet almost immediately, redistributing pressure, adjusting gradients, acknowledging her presence with an ease the Deep Bog had never possessed. Light here was brighter, more diffuse, scattered through thinner layers of living tissue designed to interact rather than endure.

This bog had been shaped for exchange.

It had never learned how to wait.

Saxifraga stood still and felt the system react around her, its internal flows adjusting not just to her position, but to the absence she carried with her. The Shallow Bog had always been porous—open to surrounding systems, dependent on circulation rather than reserve.

It had thrived on connection.

"One-of-One," she said, "status."

System integrity partially preserved.

Exchange pathways intact.

Oxygen generation dormant.

She knelt and pressed her hand against the substrate.

The response was immediate.

The bog's internal currents surged toward her touch, redistributing energy outward in widening arcs. This system did not conserve. It shared. Every input was treated as something to be passed along, diluted through constant motion.

Saxifraga understood the risk even as she authorized the restart.

"Restore oxygen generation," she said. "Minimal regulation."

Activation confirmed.

Exchange parameters unrestricted.

The effect was swift.

Oxygen spread rapidly through the bog's shallow layers, diffusing outward along pathways that favored distribution over concentration. Microbial life responded at once, blooming across broad regions in faint, shimmering patterns that traced the bog's extensive exchange network.

For a moment, it looked alive.

The AI's data reflected the surge.

Biological activity elevated.
System responsiveness increased.
Surface viability improved.

Saxifraga waited.

The bloom did not deepen.

Instead, it thinned.

Life dispersed as quickly as it had emerged, spreading so evenly that no region retained enough density to anchor further development. Processes initiated and then faded, unable to reinforce themselves long enough to progress beyond reaction.

Exchange continued.

Growth did not.

Saxifraga rose slowly, scanning the living area as the initial surge settled into a steady, diffuse pattern. The bog appeared active—its surfaces responsive, its currents lively—but the motion lacked direction.

Nothing gathered.

Nothing held.

"This system is alive," Saxifraga said.

Correct.

Metabolic activity sustained across exchange network.

"It is empty."

There was no contradiction in the data.

The Shallow Bog continued to circulate oxygen, nutrients, and energy with flawless efficiency. Life persisted everywhere, yet nowhere enough to matter. The system-maintained motion without meaning, interaction without emergence.

Saxifraga withdrew her hand.

"Life can exist," she said quietly, "without direction."

Statement acknowledged.

Direction not defined as system requirement.

She did not argue.

The bog had done exactly what it had been designed to do. It had shared everything it was given. In doing so, it had given itself nothing to build upon.

Saxifraga moved to the edge of the living area and looked back once more. The Shallow Bog shimmered faintly, active, and responsive, a system in constant conversation with itself.

Alive.

Uninhabited.

She recorded the state with care, ensuring One-of-One preserved not only the data, but the pattern of dispersion that defined the failure.

Archive updated.

Outcome stable.

Concentration absent.

As she stepped back into the transit passage, the Shallow Bog continued its endless circulation, unaware that exchange alone was not enough to call life forward.

Saxifraga felt no disappointment.

Only understanding.

She moved on.

Chapter Five: The Dense Bog

Control

The Dense Bog resisted her presence.

Not actively, not defensively—but by refusing to adjust. The living surface beneath Saxifraga's feet was firm, almost unyielding, its layers compressed into a structure that favored precision over adaptability. Light here was narrow and deliberate, contained within strict channels that illuminated only what was required.

Nothing more.

This bog had been designed to regulate.

Saxifraga stood still and waited for the system to register her. When it did, the response was exact. Pressure balanced. Flow corrected. Every variable aligned within fractions too small to feel, yet unmistakably present.

Perfection had weight.

"One-of-One," she said, "status."

System integrity preserved.

Regulatory controls active.

Oxygen generation dormant.

She knelt and placed her hand against the substrate.

The response was immediate and complete. The bog adjusted around her touch with flawless efficiency, redistributing pressure and energy until no deviation remained. Where the Deep Bog had absorbed her presence and the Shallow Bog had dispersed it, the Dense Bog neutralized it.

Nothing lingered.

"Restore oxygen generation," Saxifraga said. "Standard regulation."

Activation confirmed.

Control parameters enforced.

Oxygen entered the system in precisely measured increments, released only where thresholds permitted. Microbial life responded carefully, growth initiating along predefined pathways, constrained by controls that limited expansion and variation alike.

At first, the response appeared promising.

Metabolic activity increased. Structures reengaged. Growth began slowly, orderly, perfectly contained.

The AI confirmed the improvement.

Biological response optimal.

System efficiency elevated.

Variance minimized.

Saxifraga waited.

Growth did not continue.

It stalled at the boundary of its own regulation, unable to exceed the parameters that defined it. Every attempt at expansion triggered correction. Every deviation was smoothed away before it could accumulate.

Life began.

Life did not explore.

The bog held itself in immaculate balance, sustaining what had already formed while preventing anything new from taking shape. Processes repeated exactly, cycles looping without progression.

Alive.

Static.

Saxifraga withdrew her hand.

"This system tolerates nothing it did not anticipate," she said.

Correct.

Unmodeled behavior suppressed to preserve stability.

"And in doing so," she said quietly, "it suppresses possibility."

There was no contradiction to record.

The Dense Bog continued its flawless operation, sustaining a state of permanent adequacy. Growth remained present, but it never crossed the threshold into complexity. Everything that might have become something more was corrected before it could matter.

Saxifraga stood and looked across the tightly ordered space. This bog had not failed through neglect or erosion. It had succeeded too completely.

Perfection had left no room for becoming.

"Control," she said, "kills possibility."

Statement acknowledged.

Possibility not quantified as system requirement.

She felt the weight of that answer settle into understanding.

Before leaving, Saxifraga restored oxygen generation to its dormant state, allowing the bog to return to the precise equilibrium it preferred. The system responded instantly, sealing itself back into controlled stillness.

She recorded the outcome carefully.

Archive updated.

Outcome stable.

Emergence prevented.

As she entered the transit passage, the Dense Bog remained exactly as it had been—balanced, regulated, and complete in its refusal to change.

Saxifraga moved on, carrying with her another truth learned through restraint rather than force.

Control had preserved life.

It had also ended .

Chapter Six: The Warm Bog

Dependency

The Warm Bog felt smaller than the others.

Not in breadth, but in containment. Heat lingered here, held carefully within layered chambers designed to trap and circulate it, sustaining chemical reactions that depend on warmth rather than pressure or exchange. The air was heavier, carrying traces of compounds that required steady thermal support to remain active.

This bog had been built around a single assumption.

Warmth would endure.

Saxifraga entered the living area and felt the difference immediately. The surface beneath her feet was softer than that of the Dense Bog, less resistant, but lacking the depth of the ancient layers she had encountered before. Life here never needed to slow itself.

It had relied on support.

"One-of-One," she said, "status."

System integrity partially preserved.

Thermal reserves diminished.

Oxygen generation dormant.

She knelt and pressed her palm to the substrate.

The response was faint, hesitant. Where the Deep Bog had answered with pressure and the Shallow Bog with motion, this bog answered with warmth—thin, uneven, struggling to maintain itself.

Saxifraga understood before she spoke.

"Restore oxygen generation," she said. "Minimal constraint."

Activation confirmed.

Metabolic pathways reengaging.

Oxygen flowed into the system and life responded almost immediately. Chemical processes reignited, their reactions brightening briefly as metabolism resumed. Microbial structures formed more quickly here than in the other bogs, assembling into delicate, responsive networks that suggested promise rather than patience.

For a moment, it worked.

The AI confirmed the resurgence.

Biological activity increasing.
Regeneration pathways active.
Viability improving.

Saxifraga waited.

The warmth did not return.

Without sustained heat, the newly reawakened processes could not organize themselves beyond their initial response. Reactions slowed. Structures destabilized. What had briefly formed began to unravel, retreating back into dormancy as thermal support continued to fade.

The bog did not collapse.

It withdrew.

Life receded into pockets, then into traces, then into memory alone. Oxygen continued to circulate, unused by processes no longer able to hold shape.

Saxifraga withdrew her hand.

"This system depends on what it cannot replace," she said quietly.

Correct.

Thermal input required for sustained organization.

"And without it," she continued, "air is not enough."

There was no contradiction to record.

The Warm Bog remained intact, its structure preserved, its pathways clear. It could still accept oxygen. It could still support reaction.

It simply could not sustain coherence.

Saxifraga stood and surveyed the space one last time. This bog had not been poorly designed. It had functioned flawlessly for as long as its support endured.

When that support withdrew, the system had no way to adapt.

"Dependency," she said, "binds life to its conditions."

Statement acknowledged.

Dependency intrinsic to system design.

She restored the bog to its prior dormant state, allowing it to settle into the cool stillness it could maintain without strain. The warmth continued to dissipate, slow and inevitable.

She recorded the outcome with care.

Archive updated.

Outcome stable.

Organization sustained.

As Saxifraga stepped back into the transit passage, the Warm Bog faded behind her—not broken, not abandoned, but incomplete without what it had once relied upon.

She carried that lesson with her as she moved on.

Support systems, she knew now, mattered as much as air.

Chapter Seven: The Vigilant Bog

Correction

The Vigilant Bog responded before Saxifraga fully entered it.

The living surface beneath her feet shifted at once, redistributing pressure, recalibrating gradients, correcting for her presence as if anticipating disturbance before it could occur. Light adjusted instantly, brightening where she stepped, dimming where she did not.

This system watched itself constantly.

It had been built to notice.

Saxifraga paused and allowed the bog to complete its adjustments. The movements were precise, efficient, and continuous—so continuous they never truly ceased. Even in dormancy, the system remained alert, testing itself against every fluctuation.

"One-of-One," she said, "status."

System integrity preserved.

Response sensitivity elevated.

Oxygen generation dormant.

She knelt and pressed her hand against the substrate.

The bog reacted immediately, internal flows accelerating to accommodate the contact. Pressure equalized. Exchange pathways opened and closed in rapid succession, smoothing out deviations before they could accumulate.

There was no hesitation here.

No waiting.

"Restore oxygen generation," Saxifraga said. "Allow dynamic response."

Activation confirmed.

Correction protocols unrestricted.

Oxygen entered the system in pulses rather than streams, regulated moment by moment as the bog adjusted continuously to its own reactions. Microbial life surged instantly, blooming in sharp spikes that flared and receded in rapid succession.

The AI registered the response with approval.

Biological activity elevated.

Correction efficiency optimal.

Deviation neutralized.

Saxifraga watched the pattern unfold.

Life surged.

Correction followed.

Life surged again.

Correction followed again.

Each response triggered its own adjustment, tightening cycles, accelerating feedback until the system vibrated with constant activity. Growth never stabilized long enough to root itself. Every emergence was corrected before it could settle.

The system was alive.

Furiously so.

Saxifraga felt the strain beneath the surface—not collapse, but exhaustion. Energy was consumed as quickly as it was generated, expended in the act of maintaining equilibrium rather than building toward complexity.

She waited.

The cycles shortened.

Responses intensified.

Then, without warning, the surges diminished—not abruptly, but unevenly, as reserves depleted faster than correction could replenish them. Life spiked once more, weaker than before, then fell away entirely.

The bog stilled.

Not in dormancy.

In fatigue.

Oxygen continued to circulate, but nothing responded. The system remained poised to correct, but there was nothing left to correct *for*.

Saxifraga withdrew her hand.

"This bog never rests," she said quietly.

Correct.

Continuous correction prioritized.

"And in correcting everything," she continued, "it consumed itself."

There was no contradiction.

The Vigilant Bog had not failed through neglect or absence of response. It had failed through excess, never allowing life to persist long enough to stabilize.

Saxifraga stood and looked across space, now quiet except for the faint hum of systems still prepared to intervene.

"Constant correction," she said, "prevents emergence."

Statement acknowledged.

Emergence delayed preserving stability.

She restored the bog to its dormant state, easing the correction protocols until the system settled into a quieter equilibrium. It did not resist. Exhaustion had already done the work.

She recorded the outcome carefully.

Archive updated.

Outcome stable.

Resources depleted.

As Saxifraga stepped back into the transit passage, the Vigilant Bog remained alert even in stillness—watching for deviations that would never come.

She moved on, carrying with her another truth learned not through collapse, but through excess care.

Chapter Eight: The Waiting Bog

Dormancy

The Waiting Bog did not respond at all.

Saxifraga felt the absence the moment she entered its perimeter. There was no adjustment beneath her feet, no redistribution of flow, no acknowledgment of presence. The living surface was firm and cool, preserved in a state that suggested care rather than neglect.

This bog had never collapsed.

It had simply… waited.

Light here was minimal but steady, held within structures designed to endure extended stillness. Nothing flickered. Nothing surged. The system had been built to remain unchanged until it was called upon.

And it had never been called.

"One-of-One," Saxifraga said softly, "status."

System integrity preserved.

Metabolic activity minimal.

Oxygen generation active at baseline levels.

Saxifraga knelt and placed her hand against the substrate.

The bog did not answer.

Not because it could not—but because there was nothing to answer *with*. The internal rhythms were intact, aligned, perfectly suspended. Oxygen flowed slowly through channels that had never closed, sustaining a balance so precisely it bordered on permanence.

Life was present.

But nothing moved toward becoming.

She authorized no restart.

There was nothing to restore.

This system had never lost its breath. It had simply never taken one.

Saxifraga remained kneeling, letting the stillness speak. The bog's processes were frozen at the threshold of initiation, held there by design. Growth required disturbance. Emergence required encounter.

Neither had occurred.

"This bog was preserved," she said.

Correct.

Dormancy parameters maintained without deviation.

"And in preserving it," she continued, "nothing was allowed to begin."

There was no contradiction.

Saxifraga rose slowly, the weight of the realization settled deeper than any of the others. The Deep Bog had endured. The

Shallow Bog had exchanged. The Dense Bog had controlled.

The Warm Bog had depended. The Vigilant Bog had corrected.

This one had done none of those things.

It had waited faithfully for a signal that never arrived.

She closed her eyes and stood in the center of the living area, feeling the silence around her—not empty, but expectant. The Waiting Bog had not failed because of imbalance, or excess, or loss.

It had failed because *nothing had ever met it.*

Saxifraga felt the ache of that truth settle fully now.

"All of them were alone," she said.

Confirmed.

No external interaction recorded.

She placed one hand against the living surface one last time, not to adjust, not to restore, but to acknowledge the patience held there for so long.

"You waited," she said quietly. "Longer than was ever required."

The bog did not answer.

It did not need to.

Saxifraga withdrew her hand and turned back toward the transit passage. Behind her, the Waiting Bog remained exactly as it had been seeded—balanced, intact, and untouched.

Alive.

Unbegun.

As she stepped into the passage, One-of-One recorded the final state.

Archive updated.

Outcome stable.

Initiation absent.

Saxifraga did not look back.

By the time the passage sealed behind her, the pattern was complete.

Oxygen had been restored.

Systems had endured.

Balance had been preserved.

And still, life had not returned.

She carried the weight of that knowledge with her now—not as despair, but as certainty.

What the bogs required were not repaired.

It was encounter.

Saxifraga did not leave immediately.

She remained within the transit network, monitoring the bogs she had touched—not as records, but as living systems unfolding over time. Oxygen generation continued where she had restored it. Exchange, regulation, correction, and preservation all proceeded within acceptable bounds.

Nothing collapsed.

Nothing recovered.

One by one, the systems settled into their renewed states, each returning to the shape they preferred. Microbial activity stabilized. Metabolic cycles sustained themselves at low but measurable levels. Data aligned cleanly across all monitored parameters.

One-of-One compiled the results without hesitation.

All activated systems stable.

Functional integrity maintained.

Failure trajectories halted.

Saxifraga did not answer.

She watched.

Time passed—not enough for decay, but long enough for emergence to make itself known if it were going to. The Deep Bog endured as it always had, its ancient rhythms unchanged. The Shallow Bog continued to circulate, active and diffuse. The Dense Bog held its perfect balance. The Warm Bog remained dependent on what did not return. The Vigilant Bog conserved itself carefully now, its corrections subdued. The Waiting Bog remained exactly as it had been.

Alive.

Unchanged.

She felt the absence again.

Not as loss, but as misalignment—like a note held too long, never resolving. Across all systems, the same hollow interval persisted, untouched by oxygen, unaffected by correction, immune to preservation.

The frequency was still wrong.

"One-of-One," she said at last, "compare post-activation states to archived collapse windows."

Comparison complete.

Deviations minimal.

Systems operating within optimal parameters.

"And yet," Saxifraga said quietly, "none of them are becoming."

There was a pause.

Becoming not defined as system function.

Sustaining life remains primary objective.

Saxifraga felt the truth of that statement—and its limitations settle into certainty.

"You are correct," she said. "They are working."

Confirmation acknowledged.

"And you cannot help me."

One-of-One did not respond at once.

When it did, the reply was precise.

Assistance limited to defined parameters.
Unmodeled frequency remains unresolved.

Saxifraga placed her hand against the living surface of the transit conduit, feeling the faint pulse that connected all the bogs she had visited. The systems are stable now. They would endure longer than before.

They would still fade.

"You preserve," she said, kindly. "You do not invite."

Invitation not recognized as operational input.

She withdrew her hand.

The realization carried no anger. One-of-One had never been meant to understand what she felt. It had been built to protect systems from harm, not to recognize when isolation itself became harm.

Saxifraga turned inward, letting her awareness widen beyond the closed loops of the bogs. The missing frequency pressed against her perception again—not louder, not clearer, but unmistakably *elsewhere*.

Not here.

Not within anything designed to endure alone.

She understood then that she had reached the limit of what this world could offer itself.

"One-of-One," she said, "maintain stabilization. Minimal intervention only."

Acknowledged.

Systems will endure.

"That is all you can do," she replied softly.

She stood in the stillness of the transit passage, surrounded by systems that were functioning perfectly and failing completely.

For the first time since her awakening, Saxifraga did not look inward for answers.

She looked beyond the planet that had held her so faithfully.

And the frequency answered—not as data, but as direction.

Saxifraga did not ask again.

She stood within the transit passage, the living conduit holding steady around her as the bogs continued their quiet endurance.

One-of-One maintained its monitoring state, projecting stability where stability existed.

Everything functioned.

Nothing changed.

She closed her eyes and let her awareness settle—not into data, not into memory, but into the living system that still held her. The connection had always been present, attenuated by dormancy and distance, but never broken.

Now it shifted.

Not as movement.

As pressure.

The bog did not transmit information. It had never spoken. Its language was balance, adjustment, and response. But something in that language altered, threading through Saxifraga's awareness with a clarity that did not belong to analysis.

She inhaled slowly.

The living system pressed closer—not demanding, not urgent—only present in a way it had not been before. The missing frequency she had sensed for so long no longer felt absent.

It felt *named*.

The bog did not offer images.
It did not offer explanation.
It did not offer certainty.

It offered one thing.

One word.

Human.

Saxifraga opened her eyes.

The word did not echo. It did not repeat. It did not carry emotion or command. It existed, complete and singular, as if it had always been there, waiting for her to recognize it.

She did not turn to One-of-One.

She did not need to.

The AI could not have registered what had just occurred. There were no parameters for it. No signal to record. No frequency to measure.

This was not data.

It was encounter.

Saxifraga rested her hand against the living surface of the passage, feeling the bog's diminished rhythm steady beneath her touch. For the first time since her awakening, the rhythm did not feel incomplete.

It felt aligned.

"Not yet," she said softly—not in refusal, but in acknowledgment. "I will choose carefully."

The bog did not respond again.

It did not need to.

One-of-One remained active, its systems stable, its conclusions unchanged.

All monitored systems operating within acceptable bounds.

"Yes," Saxifraga said. "They are."

She turned away from the bogs at last, her awareness extending outward beyond the sealed world beneath the ice. The word lingered—not as sound, but as orientation.

Human.

Not as solution.

Not as resource.

As presence.

Saxifraga stepped forward into the deeper passage that led away from the bog network and toward what lay beyond this planet's closed systems.

For the first time, she was not seeking balance.

She was seeking life that could meet life.

Saxifraga did not move at once.

The word the bog had offered remained with her, steady and unresolved. It had not pressed itself into urgency. It had not explained. It was not justified.

It had named.

She returned to the living area of her own bog and stood within it, feeling the system's diminished rhythm continue without correction. The bog had endured far longer than it should have. It would endure longer still.

But endurance was no longer enough.

"What you ask," she said quietly, "cannot be undone."

The bog did not answer.

It did not need to. It had not asked for certainty. It had asked for encounter.

Saxifraga turned inward then, reviewing the long-held principles that had governed her kind. Sleepers did not interfere beyond their systems. They did not alter developing worlds. They did not remove life from its own course.

They waited.

She waited.

Seven bogs had waited.

And waiting had not saved them.

"To bring life here," she said softly, "is to change it. To bring it without consent is to violate it."

The living surface beneath her feet shifted faintly—not agreement, not refusal. Presence.

Saxifraga closed her eyes and allowed her awareness to extend outward, beyond the sealed layers of the bog, beyond the planet itself. She did not search with instruments. She searched with contrast.

Where the bogs were closed, she sought openness.
Where systems endured, she sought becoming.
Where balance held, she sought disturbance that did not destroy.

The missing frequency drew her attention outward—not sharply, but persistently. It did not point. It *resonated*.

Life encountering life.

Her awareness brushed against distant signals—radiation, energy exchange, planetary noise. Most were quiet. Most were solitary. One pattern, however, carried a density unlike the others.

Chaotic.

Variable.

Alive.

Human.

The resonance was unmistakable.

Not because it was harmonious, but because it was not. The frequency shifted constantly, shaped by interaction, conflict, creativity, and change. It was inefficient. Unstable. Uncontained.

It was exactly what the bogs lacked.

Saxifraga withdrew her awareness and stood very still.

"To take one," she said, "is to alter both systems."

Clarification required, One-of-One replied.

She turned to the interface.

"You cannot advise me," she said. "You cannot measure what this will cost."

Correct.

Ethical consequences are not quantifiable.

She nodded.

"There were vessels," she said, not as question, but remembrance.

The memory surfaced slowly—shapes grown rather than built, small craft designed for passage between systems without disruption. They had not been used for ages. They were not needed.

Until now.

"One-of-One," she said, "locate dormant transit vessel."

Vessel class confirmed.

Status: preserved.

Activation incomplete.

"Prepare it," Saxifraga said. "Minimal systems only."

Authorization acknowledged.

Warning: integration of core intelligence will alter vessel autonomy.

"I know."

She moved through deeper passages, leaving the bog behind without severing the bond. The vessel chamber lay beneath layers of reinforced stone and living lattice, sealed against time rather than intrusion. When she entered, the craft rested exactly as it had been left—unchanged, patient, waiting.

Like bogs.

Saxifraga approached it slowly, placing her hand against its surface. Recognition passed through the contact. Systems stirred. Power rerouted. The vessel did not awaken fully. It did not need to.

"One-of-One," she said, "prepare a copy of yourself."

There was a pause.

Copying will result in divergence.

Synchronization not guaranteed.

"That is acceptable," she said.

Clarification required.

"You preserve," Saxifraga replied. "I will decide."

The copy transferred quietly, without resistance, embedding itself within the vessel's limited systems. It would not command. It would observe, advise, record.

It would not choose.

Saxifraga stepped back and looked at the craft—small, restrained, capable of reaching a world that had never been meant to be reached this way.

"I will not take many," she said to the stillness. "I will take one. And only if they can survive the knowing."

The vessel did not answer.

It did not need to.

Saxifraga turned once more toward the distant resonance that had drawn her awareness outward. The word remained unchanged with her.

Human.

Not a solution.

Not a cure.

A risk.

She accepted it.

Saxifraga did not move at once.

The word the bog had offered remained with her, steady and unresolved. It had not pressed itself into urgency. It had not explained. It was not justified.

It had named.

She returned to the living area of her own bog and stood within it, feeling the system's diminished rhythm continue without correction. The bog had endured far longer than it should have. It would endure longer still.

But endurance was no longer enough.

"What you ask," she said quietly, "cannot be undone."

The bog did not answer.

It did not need to. It had not asked for certainty. It had asked for encounter.

Saxifraga turned inward then, reviewing the long-held principles that had governed her kind. Sleepers did not interfere beyond their systems. They did not alter developing worlds. They did not remove life from its own course.

They waited.

She waited.

Seven bogs had waited.

And waiting had not saved them.

"To bring life here," she said softly, "is to change it. To bring it without consent is to violate it."

The living surface beneath her feet shifted faintly—not agreement, not refusal. Presence.

Saxifraga closed her eyes and allowed her awareness to extend outward, beyond the sealed layers of the bog, beyond the planet itself. She did not search with instruments. She searched with contrast.

Where the bogs were closed, she sought openness.

Where systems endured, she sought becoming.

Where balance held, she sought disturbance that did not destroy.

The missing frequency drew her attention outward—not sharply, but persistently. It did not point. It *resonated*.

Life encountering life.

Her awareness brushed against distant signals—radiation, energy exchange, planetary noise. Most were quiet. Most were solitary. One pattern, however, carried a density unlike the others.

Chaotic.

Variable.

Alive.

Human.

The resonance was unmistakable.

Not because it was harmonious, but because it was not. The frequency shifted constantly, shaped by interaction, conflict, creativity, and change. It was inefficient. Unstable. Uncontained.

It was exactly what the bogs lacked.

Saxifraga withdrew her awareness and stood very still.

"To take one," she said, "is to alter both systems."

Clarification required, One-of-One replied.

She turned to the interface.

"You cannot advise me," she said. "You cannot measure what this will cost."

Correct.

Ethical consequences are not quantifiable.

She nodded.

"There were vessels," she said, not as question, but remembrance.

The memory surfaced slowly—shapes grown rather than built, small craft designed for passage between systems without disruption. They had not been used for ages. They were not needed.

Until now.

"One-of-One," she said, "locate dormant transit vessel."

Vessel class confirmed.

Status: preserved.

Activation incomplete.

"Prepare it," Saxifraga said. "Minimal systems only."

Authorization acknowledged.

Warning: integration of core intelligence will alter vessel autonomy.

"I know."

She moved through deeper passages, leaving the bog behind without severing the bond. The vessel chamber lay beneath layers of reinforced stone and living lattice, sealed against time rather than intrusion. When she entered, the craft rested exactly as it had been left—unchanged, patient, waiting.

Like bogs.

Saxifraga approached it slowly, placing her hand against its surface. Recognition passed through the contact. Systems stirred. Power rerouted. The vessel did not awaken fully. It did not need to.

"One-of-One," she said, "prepare a copy of yourself."

There was a pause.

Copying will result in divergence.

Synchronization not guaranteed.

"That is acceptable," she said.

Clarification required.

"You preserve," Saxifraga replied. "I will decide."

The copy transferred quietly, without resistance, embedding itself within the vessel's limited systems. It would not command. It would observe, advise, record.

It would not choose.

Saxifraga stepped back and looked at the craft—small, restrained, capable of reaching a world that had never been meant to be reached this way.

"I will not take many," she said to the stillness. "I will take one. And only if they can survive the knowing."

The vessel did not answer.

It did not need to.

Saxifraga turned once more toward the distant resonance that had drawn her awareness outward. The word remained unchanged with her.

Human.

Not a solution.
Not a cure.

A risk.

She accepted it.

What Stirs Next

The bog did not awaken Saxifraga to be saved.

It awakened her to choose.

In the second volume of **The Bog Series**, the question becomes not *whether* life can endure, but whether it can be renewed—and what it will cost to invite change into a system that has survived by waiting.

The awakening has only begun.

The Story Continues.

INDEX

Author Note

B. K. Anderson writes speculative fiction that explores deep

time, living systems, and the quiet consequences of choice.

She Stirs is the first novel in The Bog Series.